# The Best Kind of Bear

Greg Gormley & David Barrow

# The Best Kind of Bear

nosy crow

Bear was a bear. A very sweet little bear.
But he didn't know what **kind** of bear he was.

One day, he met a small child.

"Hello, I'm Nelly," she said.
"What kind of bear are you?"

"That's what I'm trying to find out," said Bear.
"Maybe there's a bear out there who can help me."

"Good luck!" said Nelly.
"Will you come back and tell me?"

GRIZZLY
BEAR
HOME: NORTH AMERICA

SPECTACLED
BEAR
HOME: SOUTH AMERICA

PO     AR
HOM

SUN

"Yes," said Bear,
and off he went.

First, Bear travelled west.
Deep in the forest he met a big brown bear.

"What kind of bear are you?" asked Bear.

"I'm a grizzly bear," said the big brown bear.
"I love nice long naps."

"Me too," said Bear. "I love napping."

Grizzly Bear stretched and yawned.
"Fancy a nap then?" he said.

"I do love snoozing," said Bear.
"Maybe I'm a grizzly bear."

"Jolly good," said Grizzly Bear.
"Wake me up in six months."

"What?" said Bear. "That's too much sleep and not enough fun. I can't possibly be a grizzly bear."

"Maybe not," said Grizzly Bear. "Besides, grizzly bears don't have those funny little stitches on their tummies."

Next, Bear travelled to the frozen north. There, he found an even bigger bear. It was completely white.

"What kind of bear are you?" asked Bear.

"I'm a polar bear," said the big white bear. "I like to play in the snow."

"Me too," said Bear. "I love playing."

The two bears went snowsliding.
"This is fun," said Bear. "Maybe I'm a polar bear."

Bear was starting to feel chilly.
"Shall we go inside and get nice and toasty?"
he asked.

"I never ever go inside," said Polar Bear.

"Brrr," said Bear. "I like to be cosy.
I can't possibly be a polar bear."

"Maybe not," said Polar Bear.
"Besides, polar bears don't have
washing labels attached to
their bottoms."

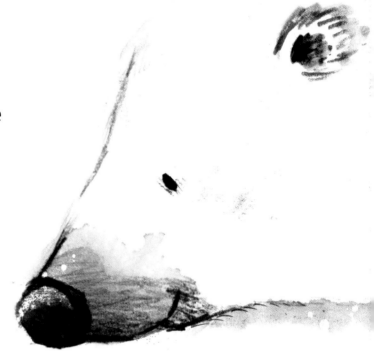

This time, Bear tried the sunny south.
There, he met a bear with long,
useful-looking claws.

"What kind of bear are you?" asked Bear.

"I'm a spectacled bear," said the bear
with the long claws. "I love to climb."

"Me too," said Bear. "Most of all,
I love climbing into bed.
Maybe I'm a spectacled bear."

"Come on then," said Spectacled Bear
as he scrambled up a very tall tree.

"Oh, right, OK," said Bear,
following carefully.

"Ooh, the view is pretty," said Bear.
But then he looked down.

"I feel a little dizzy,"
said Bear, and . . .

"Aaaah!"

He fell off the branch
and down from the tree.

BIFF,

BONK,

**BUMP!**

"Ow!" said Bear.
"I do not like climbing!
I can't possibly be a spectacled bear."

"Maybe not," said Spectacled Bear.
"Besides, spectacled bears are not
as soft and bouncy as you."

Finally, Bear travelled east to another forest,
where he met the cutest bear yet.

"What kind of bear are you?" asked Bear.

"I'm a sun bear," said the very cute bear.
"I love honey, honey, honey."

"Me too," said Bear. "I love eating honey at a picnic.
I must be a sun bear. But where do you get the honey from?"

"From that nest," said Sun Bear. "Get ready to . . .

# . . . RUN!"

The two bears ran over logs and under bushes, until . . .

. . . SPLASH!
They jumped into a river.

"Dear me," spluttered Bear. "I don't like bees and I don't like getting wet, so I'm **definitely** not a sun bear."

"Maybe not," said Sun Bear. "Besides, sun bears never wear **bow ties**."

Bear felt fed up. He decided it was time to go home.

Nelly was waiting there for him.
"What did you find out?" she said.

"Well," said Bear . . .
"I love naps,
but not ones that are too long.

And I love playing,
but only where it's warm and cosy.

I love climbing into bed,
but I do not like climbing trees,

and although I love honey,
I do not like getting wet.
And I definitely do not like bees!

But I still don't know what kind of bear I am.
I suppose that I'm just any old bear, quite
ordinary and uninteresting."

"You're a wonderful kind of bear!"
said Nelly. "A bear who has . . .

funny little stitches and
a washing label on his bottom,
who is soft and bouncy, and who
wears a very smart bow tie."

"I am?" said Bear.

"Yes," said Nelly. "You're my kind of bear and you belong with me. You can be my bear, if you'd like to."

"Do you know," said Bear, "I think I would."

And so Nelly wrote on Bear's label . . .

Nelly's Bear.

"That's what kind of bear I am," said Bear.
"I'm your bear . . .

and that's the very best kind of bear to be."

For Mom – G.G.
For Caleb and Eli – D.B.

First published 2019 by Nosy Crow Ltd, The Crow's Nest,
14 Baden Place, Crosby Row, London SE1 1YW
www.nosycrow.com

ISBN 978 1 78800 203 5 (HB)
ISBN 978 1 78800 204 2 (PB)

Nosy Crow and associated logos are trademarks and/or registered trademarks
of Nosy Crow Ltd.

Text © Greg Gormley 2019
Illustrations © David Barrow 2019

A CIP catalogue record for this book is available from the British Library.

Papers used by Nosy Crow are made from wood grown in sustainable forests.

1 3 5 7 9 10 8 6 4 2  (HB)
1 3 5 7 9 10 8 6 4 2  (PB)